HEIDI HECKELBECK

and the Wild Ride

By Wanda Coven
Illustrated by Priscilla Burris

LITTLE SIMON

New York London Toronto Sydney New Delhi

LITTLE SIMON
An imprint of Simon & Schuster Children's Publishing Division
1230 Avenue of the Americas, New York, New York 10020
First Little Simon paperback edition December 2021
Copyright © 2021 by Simon & Schuster, Inc.
Also available in a Little Simon hardcover edition.
All rights reserved, including the right of reproduction in whole or in part in any form. LITTLE SIMON is a registered trademark of Simon & Schuster, Inc., and associated colophon is a trademark of Simon & Schuster, Inc. For information about special discounts for bulk purchases, please contact Simon & Schuster Special Sales at 1-866-506-1949 or business@simonandschuster.com.
The Simon & Schuster Speakers Bureau can bring authors to your live event. For more information or to book an event contact the Simon & Schuster Speakers Bureau at 1-866-248-3049 or visit our website at www.simonspeakers.com.
Designed by Chani Yammer
Manufactured in the United States of America 1121 MTN
10 9 8 7 6 5 4 3 2 1
Library of Congress Cataloging-in-Publication Data
Names: Coven, Wanda, author. | Burris, Priscilla, illustrator.
Title: Heidi Heckelbeck and the wild ride / by Wanda Coven ; illustrated by Priscilla Burris.
Description: First Little Simon paperback edition. | New York : Little Simon, 2021. | Series: Heidi Heckelbeck ; 34 | Summary: Heidi takes a road trip with her best friend Lucy Lancaster to the Wacky Wonders Adventure Park where there are waterslides, wild rides, and plenty of friendship drama between Heidi and Lucy.
Identifiers: LCCN 2021028368 (print) | LCCN 2021028369 (ebook) | ISBN 9781665911283 (paperback) | ISBN 9781665911290 (hardcover) | ISBN 9781665911306 (ebook)
Subjects: CYAC: Witches—Fiction. | Friendship—Fiction. | Amusement parks—Fiction.
Classification: LCC PZ7.C83393 Hbx 2021 (print) | LCC PZ7.C83393 (ebook) | DDC [Fic]—dc23
LC record available at https://lccn.loc.gov/2021028368
LC ebook record available at https://lccn.loc.gov/2021028369

CONTENTS

Chapter 1

IT'S ABOUT TIME!

Tick-tock!

Tick-tock!

Heidi and her best friend Lucy Lancaster stared at the clock in their classroom. Their teacher Mrs. Welli had given the class Choice Time until the end of the day.

The girls had chosen to watch the clock.

"Our THREE-DAY weekend starts in a few minutes!" said Heidi.

Lucy muffled a squeal with the palm of her hand.

Bruce Bickerson sat across from the girls. He was reading a book called *All About Snakes*.

"What are you guys doing?" he asked.

"We're watching the clock until school lets out," said Heidi without looking at him.

"I can see that," said Bruce. "But why?"

This time the girls took their eyes off the clock.

"Because we're going to Wacky Wonders Adventure Park this weekend!" said Lucy.

Heidi bounced in her seat. "Yeah! It has rides, games, and an INDOOR water park!"

Lucy nodded excitedly. "Plus their Wonder Thunder roller coaster goes a hundred miles per hour AND upside down!"

Bruce's eyes widened. "COOL!" he said. "I've seen the Wacky Wonders ads on TV. Isn't it far from here?"

"Yeah," said Lucy, "but that means we're going on a ROAD TRIP!" The girls let out another squeal.

"I'm packing treats to munch on the way!" said Heidi.

Lucy rubbed her tummy. "And I'll make a playlist of cool songs and download a movie, too!"

Heidi flapped her hands excitedly. "It'll be a party on wheels! Then we stay in a hotel at the park!"

Both girls broke into the Wacky Wonders theme song. *"Come for adventure! Stay for the friends! At Wacky Wonders, the fun never ends!"*

"Sounds like a blast," said Bruce. "And by the way, you both owe me a THANK-YOU."

The girls raised their eyebrows and asked, "For what?"

Suddenly the final bell rang.

"For taking your minds off the clock," said Bruce with a laugh. "Your weekend starts now!"

Chapter 2

PACK IT!

Ka-bonk!

Ka-bonk!

Ka-bonk!

Heidi dragged her overnight bag up the stairs and into her bedroom. Then she made a packing list so she wouldn't forget a single thing.

bathing suit
flip-flops
skirts
shirts
shoes
headbands
tights
hairbrush
toothpaste
toothbrush

First she laid out her favorite palm tree bathing suit and three more outfits. She looked for matching headbands next.

Henry, her little brother, passed by in the hallway, and Heidi was in such a good mood, she waved him into her room.

Henry looked behind him to see if Heidi was talking to somebody else. "Me?" he asked.

"Yes, you," Heidi said. "I need your help. Which headband is best for a roller coaster that goes a hundred miles per hour AND upside down?"

Henry's jaw dropped. "YOU'RE going to ride a roller coaster that goes a hundred miles per hour AND goes upside down?" he asked. "Wow, you have more guts than I thought!"

Heidi gulped. Suddenly she pictured what it would be like to go upside down and *really* fast on a roller coaster. *Eek!*

"Oh, it's no big deal," she said casually. She didn't want Henry to think she was chicken.

Henry sighed dreamily. "Well, I hope a friend takes ME to Wacky Wonders someday. We'd ride everything TWICE—once with our eyes open and once with our eyes shut."

Heidi smirked. "You'd look pretty silly riding the merry-go-round with your eyes shut!"

Henry laughed. Then he tapped a finger on Heidi's stretchy purple headband.

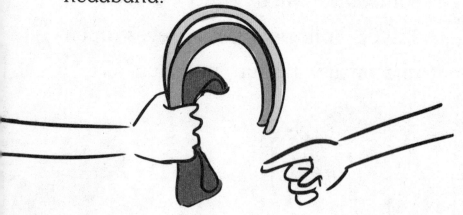

"Wear that one," he said. "It looks strong enough to keep your hair in place at a hundred miles per hour."

Heidi plucked the stretchy headband from the others.

"Good point," she said, and she stashed the headband in her suitcase.

Henry took off, and Heidi reached for her packing list. *Swoosh!* It fluttered onto the floor beside her bed.

That's weird, she thought. *My window isn't even open!*

She stooped to pick it up and noticed her *Book of Spells* under the bed.

Hmm, maybe I should pack my Book of Spells, she thought. *What if it rains? Or what if some of the best rides are closed?*

She grabbed her *Book of Spells* and buried it at the bottom of her suitcase.

It never hurts to pack a little magic . . . just in case!

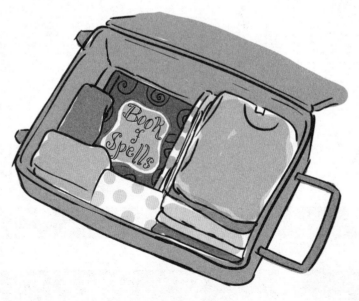

Chapter 3

BUZZKiLL!

Heidi rolled her suitcase onto the front step the next morning and sat down. Waiting for Lucy was going to be hard!

"Don't forget *these*!" Mom said as she handed Heidi a tote bag full of treats.

Heidi hugged the bag close.

"Thanks, Mom!" she cried. "How could I forget my dried mangoes, Ooey-Gooey granola bars, and snack mix with EXTRA pretzels?"

"I know!" said Mom. "After you worked so hard to pick each treat and pack them!"

Heidi jumped up and hugged Mom. At the same time, she spied the Lancasters' minivan turning onto her street.

"They're here!" she cried.

Lucy opened
the side door
and invited Heidi
inside. The girls
squealed and
scrambled into
the very back seat—
so they could be private.
Heidi's mom slid the door shut and

waved to the Lancasters. Heidi waved
good-bye to her mom.
She also waved to
Henry and Dad, who
were now standing
on the front steps in
their pajamas.

The road trip
had begun!

Lucy pulled out her tablet.

"Let's watch a movie!" she suggested. "I rented *Dolphin Dreams*! It's a movie about a dolphin who dreams he's a real kid!" She clicked on the movie icon.

"Sounds fun!" said Heidi, scooting closer to Lucy.

The girls waited for the movie to load. The little rainbow wheel circled and circled. Then a window popped up that said UH-OH! DOWNLOAD FAILED. PLEASE TRY AGAIN!

Lucy clicked the icon again. And again. The same message popped up every time.

UH-OH! DOWNLOAD FAILED. PLEASE TRY AGAIN!

"Ugh, it's not working!" she said. "Wanna listen to music instead? I made a special playlist for the ride."

Heidi loved music, so she said, "Sure!"

Lucy opened the music app and hit play. A song Heidi had never heard before came on. But Lucy knew all the words. She sang and bounced along to the song.

She even sang the refrain. It went, *"Don't worry, we got this!"*

When the song finally ended, Heidi waited for the next one. She hoped she would know this song! But then the same song started all over again!

"Uh, I think your playlist is broken," said Heidi. "It's playing the same song twice."

"Nothing's wrong. This song IS my whole playlist!" said Lucy. "Isn't it great? I could hear this song a million times!" Then she went back to singing.

And Lucy wasn't kidding.

Every time the song ended, it started again . . . over and over and over.

Heidi folded her arms and huffed loudly. But Lucy was so into her song, she didn't even notice.

"How long till we get there?" shouted Heidi over the music.

Lucy stopped singing long enough to answer, "Two hours!"

Heidi rolled her eyes and stared out the window. Suddenly two hours seemed like *forever*.

"How about a snack?" Heidi asked.

Lucy turned down the music and said, "Sounds good! What did you bring?"

Heidi opened the bag and pulled out dried mangoes.

"Ew, *mangoes!* *Gross!*" Lucy said.
"What else is here?"

Lucy grabbed a granola bar, looked
at it, and dropped it back in the bag.

"I don't like this kind. They're too
messy!"

Next she pulled out the snack mix.

"Why does this snack mix have so many pretzels?" Lucy asked. "Pretzels are the worst part! Ugh, you know, I'm not even that hungry yet. I'll eat around the pretzels later."

Then she cranked up her favorite song again.

Heidi went back to staring out the window and wondered how many times Lucy could listen to that one song.

Probably like a BAZILLION?! Merg.

Chapter 4

THE WAFFLE CURE

A giant waterslide curved out of one side of the Wacky Wonders hotel and back inside the other. Heidi and Lucy loaded their suitcases onto a rolling luggage cart. Then they went through a revolving door before they entered the lobby.

"*Mmm*, it smells like waffles in here!" cried Heidi.

"It's coming from the breakfast bar!" said Lucy, who grabbed her mom by the arm. "Can we make WAFFLES?"

Mrs. Lancaster nodded, and the girls raced to the free waffle station.

Heidi and
Lucy each took a
fresh waffle and
plopped them
onto paper plates.
Then they squirted
whipped cream on
top, along with
rainbow sprinkles
and syrup.

Heidi's mouth
watered as she
followed Lucy and
her parents to their
suite.

Waffles make everything better, Heidi thought. *Waffles and best friends, that is.*

The long car trip was behind them now. It was time to have fun!

The girls set their waffles down and explored the suite. It had a living room, a mini kitchen, and two bedrooms. The girls ran into their bedroom.

"I call the bed by the window!" cried Lucy.

Heidi jumped on the other bed. "Good! Because I like the one away from the window!"

Then they ran back to enjoy their
waffles.

"Can we go to the water park after
we eat?" Lucy asked her mom.

Lucy's mom nodded. "As soon as
you change into your bathing suits,
we can go."

The girls wiggled in their seats.

They didn't even finish their waffles.
They raced to their room and slid into
their bathing suits and flip-flops.

The girls ran down the long hallway
to the water park entrance. As soon
as they yanked open the door, a wave
of tropical air washed over them.
They stopped and stared.

Water slides twirled into the sky everywhere they looked!

"This is KID PARADISE!" cried Heidi.

The water park had a shallow pool for little kids. It was called the Guppy Zone. Then there was an adventure pool for bigger kids that had a floating trampoline, an inflatable island with a castle and slides, and a rope swing. It was called the Bass Splash Zone.

Finally there was a pool for older kids called the Shark Zone. It had a daredevil ride called the Wave Crasher.

And circling all three pools was a giant lazy river that swimmers could float in.

"Let's do the Bass Splash Zone!" said Lucy.

The girls kicked off their flip-flops, and *SPLASH!* They jumped into the water at the same time.

First they swam to
the trampoline and
bounced. Then they
slid down the slides.
They even took turns
on the rope swing.
"I'm ready to float
in the lazy river!" said Heidi.

The girls each stepped into clear
plastic inner tubes and jumped in the
river. Heidi scooped
a handful of water
and splashed
Lucy. This started
a splash war.

The inner tubes squeaked as they
bounced off each other and floated
toward the Shark Zone. Music blared,
and colored lights swirled.

"Look! It's the WAVE CRASHER!" Lucy shouted. "Let's go on THAT next!"

Heidi's stomach flip-flopped. *Uh-oh,* she thought. *The Wave Crasher doesn't sound fun at all!*

As Heidi floated closer to the Wave Crasher, she watched a rider spin around on the waves until he crashed underwater. Then a video of him falling appeared on a huge screen above the water park, and the song "Wipe Out" played.

To make matters worse, a crowd of people were watching and laughing.

Lucy paddled out of the lazy river. "Let's go!" she cried.

Heidi followed reluctantly. The girls dropped their inner tubes into a bin. Lucy grabbed Heidi by the arm and pulled her into the line. Heidi watched another rider do a belly flop on the waves.

"Uh, Lucy," Heidi whispered, "I'm going to skip this ride."

Lucy spun around and faced Heidi. "What do you MEAN?! This is a TWO-person ride!" she said. "I don't want to wipe out with somebody I don't KNOW!"

Heidi stared blankly at Lucy.

"It'll be fun. I promise!" Lucy said. "Please, Heidi. *PLEEEEEASE!* It won't be the same without you!"

Heidi finally caved. "Okay, FINE."

When it was their turn, the girls entered the pool and stood side by side on small surfboards that floated in the water. The waves began to bubble over their feet.

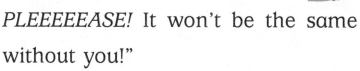

This isn't so bad, Heidi thought at first as the surfboard floated.

Then the waves grew stronger and stronger . . . until Heidi crashed.

"WIPE OUT!" boomed the voice from the overhead speakers.

Heidi swished into the safety pool and heard the "Wipe Out" song playing. She looked up at the screen and saw herself crash in slow motion!

Then Heidi was hit with *another* wave—a wave of *laughter*.

Lucy swam up to Heidi. "You're FAMOUS!" she joked.

Heidi hid her face. "Ugh, this is SO embarrassing!" she cried.

Then Heidi dove underwater and swam to get out.

Lucy called after her, "It's NOT embarrassing!" She giggled. "It's FUN!"

Heidi shook her head and said, "Not to me!"

Chapter 6

MAD RIDES

"Room service, anyone?" asked Lucy's mom, waving a menu in front of the girls.

Room service. Those two magic words made Heidi forget how mad she was about the Wave Crasher.

"Yes, please!" the girls cried.

Heidi and Lucy ordered chicken tenders, fries, and sundaes. They chose three toppings on their sundaes: toasted marshmallows, caramel sauce, and cookie crumbles.

The girls sat by the window and dipped their fries in their sundaes. Outside, the lights of Wacky Wonders twinkled magically.

"It's breathtaking," Lucy said. Then she yawned deeply.

Heidi leaned on her elbows and yawned too.

After dinner the girls brushed their teeth and crawled into bed. They fell asleep even before they said good night.

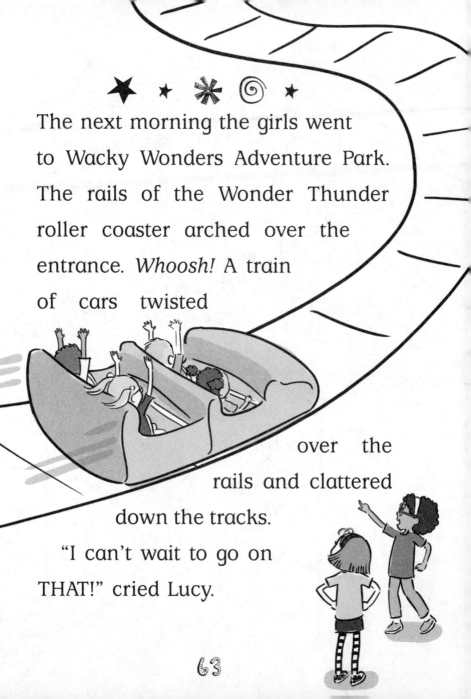

The next morning the girls went to Wacky Wonders Adventure Park. The rails of the Wonder Thunder roller coaster arched over the entrance. *Whoosh!* A train of cars twisted over the rails and clattered down the tracks.

"I can't wait to go on THAT!" cried Lucy.

Heidi looked away.
Not me, she thought.
That looks way too scary.

Lucy and Heidi
walked through the gate
and under the roller
coaster. The girls saw
kids sitting on a ride
around the tippy-top
of a high tower. Then
SWOOSH! They dropped
to the bottom of the
tower. They also saw a
Ferris wheel gently
turn round.

The girls ran straight to the Stuffed Animal Barn. Heidi bought a stuffed mouse with a rope tail. Lucy bought a stuffed chinchilla that looked totally real.

Heidi and Lucy stopped to watch hip-hop dancers stomp and shake in the middle of the park as a crowd clapped along.

Next the girls played a
Ring the Bottle game. Lucy
missed on all three tosses. But Heidi
ringed three bottles and won a *prize*.
She chose a stretchy bracelet with her
name spelled on beads.

"Now let's go on
some RIDES!" cried
Lucy. "What should
we try first?"

"How about the Ladybug Twist?" asked Heidi.

The Ladybug Twist was a twirly ride where four ladybug carts went round and round at the same time. Lucy squished Heidi every time they twirled, and the girls shrieked with laughter.

As soon as the ride ended, Lucy said, "Now let's go on the Wonder Thunder roller coaster!"

"No, thank you," said Heidi as they climbed out of the ladybug. "I'm going to skip that one."

Lucy stopped in her tracks. "But it's the ride we've been looking forward to since we began to plan our trip!"

Heidi shook her head. "No, Lucy. YOU'VE been looking forward to this ride. NOT ME."

Lucy put her hands on her hips. "What is going on with you, Heidi? First you don't like my playlist, then you almost skip out on the Wave Crasher, and NOW you're bailing on the roller coaster?!"

Heidi began to grow very hot. Then all her anger erupted like a volcano.

"What's going on with ME?" she shouted. "I'll TELL YOU what's going on with me! First you MADE me listen to the SAME song in the car a billion times! Then you couldn't even download a simple movie. And did I complain? NO! But YOU didn't like my snacks! And then you also FORCED me to go on the Wave Crasher when I didn't want to. Is that what you call being a good friend?"

Lucy clenched her fists and said, "Well, I can't help it if you're just a big CHICKEN!"

And that's when Lucy's parents stepped in between the girls.

"Lucy, you and I can go on the roller coaster," said her dad, taking her by the hand.

Mrs. Lancaster put her arm around
Heidi. "And we'll find something else
fun to do."

Heidi watched Lucy walk away
with her dad. She didn't even
look back.

And Heidi was too
mad to even care.

Chapter 7

SEWING PROJECT

Heidi and Lucy's mom rode the Swing Carousel, the Flying Banana, the Ferris wheel, and the Rattler, a smaller roller coaster that looked like a rattlesnake.

Heidi and Lucy didn't see each other until dinner.

They all met at Wacky Pizza.

A waitress led them to a table. Normally, Heidi and Lucy sat side by side. But not this time. Tonight they sat on opposite sides.

"I want pepperoni," Lucy said.

Heidi wrinkled her nose and said, "Well, I want mushroom."

Lucy's dad turned to the waitress. "Please split the toppings down the middle," he said. "My wife and I will share a veggie pizza."

The girls didn't say one word during dinner. They didn't even talk on the way back to the hotel. That night Lucy played games on her tablet, and Heidi watched a spy movie on the hotel TV.

"Bedtime, girls," Lucy's mom announced after a while.

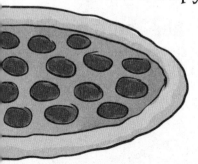

"I'm sleeping on the foldout sofa,"
Lucy told her mom.

Then she grabbed her stuffed
animal and left Heidi all alone in the
bedroom.

Heidi sighed. *Wow, this is the WORST fight Lucy and I have ever had,* she thought. *How are we ever going to get over it?*

Then Heidi had an idea. She could use her *Book of Spells*.

She grabbed it from the bottom of her suitcase and locked the bedroom door. The last thing she wanted was to get caught doing magic.

Heidi opened it to the chapter on friendship and found the Emergency Friend Spell. She read it over.

Emergency Friend Spell

Have you ever had a fight with your best friend? Maybe you don't always like the same music. Or perhaps one of you likes roller coasters and the other doesn't. Or could it be you simply can't agree on a pizza topping? If you need to sew your friendship back together, then this is the spell for YOU!

Ingredients:

1 shower cap

1 bar of soap

2 strands of thread

1 squirt of shampoo

Gather the ingredients together in the shower cap. Hold your Witches of Westwick medallion in one hand, and place your other hand over the mix. Chant the following spell:

MiX ThiS PoTioN RoUND aND RoUND.

To ThiS sPeLL yoU aRE BoUND.

LeT yoUR aNGeR MeLT aWaY.

MeND ThiS FRieNDShiP coMe WhaT MaY!

Heidi ran into the bathroom and grabbed a shower cap, a bar of soap, and a mini shampoo. She pulled two strands of purple thread from the sewing kit. Then she placed all the ingredients in the shower cap.

As Heidi chanted the spell, a warm wave of peace washed over her. She put the used spell ingredients in the wastebasket, unlocked the door, and crawled into bed, where she fell fast asleep.

Chapter 8

WAFFLE GOOD!

Heidi rubbed her eyes with the backs of her hands as she woke up. There was a very yummy smell in the air. She lifted her head to see Lucy at the foot of her bed.

Lucy smiled and pointed to a tray of waffles.

"I made all different kinds," she said, "because I was being all kinds of silly the past few days."

There were waffles with chocolate chips, waffles with maple drizzle, and waffles with whipped cream and strawberries. One plate had just bacon and sausage.

"You did this all for ME?" Heidi asked.

"Well, I woke up and missed my best friend," Lucy said. "And I kept thinking, 'Waffles make everything better!'"

Heidi kicked off the covers and added, "You mean waffles and BEST FRIENDS make everything better!"

"Exactly!" Lucy cheered.

Then the girls propped up pillows, sat beside each other, and had waffles in bed.

"I'm SO sorry," said Lucy. "I wasn't very nice when you didn't want to ride the roller coaster or the Wave Crasher."

"And I'm sorry I didn't tell you I don't like wild rides," said Heidi.

Lucy pressed her hand to her heart. "Well, I'm sorry I tortured you by playing the same song over and over in the car!"

Heidi grinned. "Well, that DID get kind of old."

And both girls burst into laughter.

"Let's make a waffle promise," said Lucy, holding up a forkful of waffle. "No more fighting with each other. Because I like you . . . a WAFFLE LOT."

Heidi held up a big bite of waffle and said, "Well, I like you a waffle lot WITH SYRUP ON TOP!" Then they tapped forks and giggled.

"Okay, we have one day left at Wacky Wonders," Lucy said. "Let's only do stuff we BOTH want to do."

Heidi set her plate back on the tray. "Deal."

"Cool!" said Lucy. "But first we need some napkins! There's syrup everywhere!"

Lucy scooted off the bed and headed to the other room. Then she paused at the door and said, "By the way, I put your book on the bedside table. You left it on the floor."

Heidi looked at her magic book. It was sitting there, right out in the open!

"Thanks," Heidi said.

She was trying to keep cool, but she couldn't help thinking, *OH NO! Did Lucy notice it was a book of SPELLS?!*

Chapter 9

WE GOT THIS!

"Let's ride the Rattler first!" Heidi suggested.

"I'm IN!" agreed Lucy.

The girls scrambled into the front seat, which had a snake's head. The ride crept toward the first hill, and then it took off down the rails.

The Rattler snaked around twists and bends and up and down hills.

"That was SO fun!" Lucy said as they coasted to a stop.

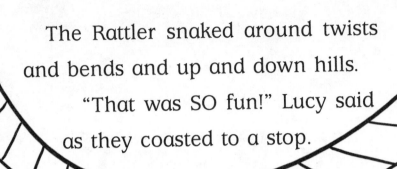

"Are you saying that to be nice?" asked Heidi.

Lucy shook her head. "No, I'm SERIOUS! The Wonder Thunder roller coaster isn't that much different. The hills and loops are just a little bigger."

Heidi gazed wide-eyed at the giant Wonder Thunder

coaster. Riders screamed as the cars whizzed by.

"But it's SO FAST!" she said.

Lucy shrugged. "The speed just makes it more fun!"

The Wonder Thunder did a loop-de-loop.

"But did you feel safe?" Heidi asked.

Lucy nodded. "Totally safe," she said.

Heidi took a deep breath and said, "Okay, then let's DO IT."

Lucy's eyes widened as she took Heidi by the hand. The girls skipped happily to the Wonder Thunder line.

When it was their turn, Heidi froze in place.

Lucy noticed and took her hand. Then she said, "Don't worry, Heidi. I'll be with you every step of the way."

That's when Heidi knew everything would be okay.

The girls sat in the middle of the train of cars. A ride operator checked their safety bars, and then the cars began to roll down the rails.

Heidi looked around as they climbed to the top of the highest hill. The view was amazing! Then—*WHOOSH!*

The cars plunged down the first drop.

"AAA-AAA-AAA!" screamed *all* the riders as the coaster roared around the tracks.

Heidi felt like her insides were floating. They lurched one way and then the other. Heidi also screamed the whole way . . . even after the cars coasted to a stop.

Then she asked, "Is it over already?"

Lucy laughed. "So, what did you think?"

"I think my mind is in SHOCK," said Heidi as both girls climbed out of the car. "But let's do it AGAIN."

Lucy screamed, "Really?!"

"Yup!" cried Heidi.

The girls rode the Wonder Thunder five times in a row.

After that they played Spin the Wheel, Gone Fishing, and Beanbag Toss. They won finger puppet critters

and a pair of socks with math problems all over them.

"Bruce will LOVE these socks," said Heidi.

Lucy nodded.
"They're perfect!"

After that the girls rode the Log Flume, the Whip, and the Zero-Gravity Roundup. They even went through the Haunted House twice.

"Want some pink cotton candy?" asked Lucy.

Heidi thought about it and said, "Hmm, I'd rather have BLUE."

The girls bolted to the cotton candy counter.

"See? We CAN agree on snacks!" said Lucy.

Heidi giggled. "Except for maybe mangoes and pretzels!"

Chapter 10

MAGiCAL

Heidi and Lucy sang the Wacky Wonders theme song all the way back to the car.

"Come for adventure! Stay for the friends! At Wacky Wonders, the fun never ends!"

Lucy's dad unlocked the car.

"Are you two going to sing that song *all* the way home?" he asked.

"Nope," said Heidi. "We've got an even BETTER song for the ride!"

"Do I dare ask how that one goes?" asked Lucy's mom as she loaded the bags.

The girls looked at each other and broke into song. *"Don't worry, we GOT this!"*

Then they burst into giggles.

Heidi and Lucy climbed into the very back seat. Lucy opened her tablet and clicked on the movie *Dolphin Dreams*. This time it worked.

"No WAY!" Lucy cried.

The two friends snuggled shoulder to shoulder so they could both see the screen. Heidi set the snacks in between them. Lucy pulled out a mango.

"I'm going to try one," she said.
"Just to see."

She nibbled a piece of dried mango,
and her face lit up. "Wow, this is
REALLY good!"

Heidi popped a piece of mango in
her mouth too. "You're totally faking."

Lucy shook her head. "No way, I'm serious! I LIKE it! I just don't like  REGULAR mangoes. They're kind of slimy. But I'll still take a pass on extra pretzels in a snack mix."

Heidi fished a pretzel from the snack bag, flipped it in the air, and caught it in her mouth.

"MORE for ME!" she said.

Then the movie started, and the girls stopped talking. One of the songs in the movie was "Don't Worry, We Got This!" Both Heidi and Lucy sang along.

"I wish our trip would last forever," said Lucy.

"Same!" Heidi agreed.

Lucy's mom turned around and asked, "Would you *really* like your trip to last forever?"

The girls looked at each other and said, "YES!"

"Then here's a little gift . . . to remember your trip forever," said Lucy's mom.

She handed her daughter a large envelope. Lucy opened it and pulled out two pictures. They were of Lucy and Heidi riding the roller coaster.

"Look! We're both screaming louder than loud!" Lucy said with a laugh.

"I'm SO glad I went on the Wonder Thunder coaster," said Heidi. "Thank you SO much for this picture, Mr. and Mrs. Lancaster, AND for the best weekend ever!"

Heidi and Lucy slung their arms around each other.

"You know what?" said Lucy. "Having a best friend is so MAGICAL."

Heidi gulped. Did Lucy use the word "magical" because she saw the spell book?!

Then Heidi thought, *Oh, WHO CARES?! Lucy's right! Having a best friend might be the most magical wonder of all!*

There's more

HEiDi HECKELBECK

to explore!